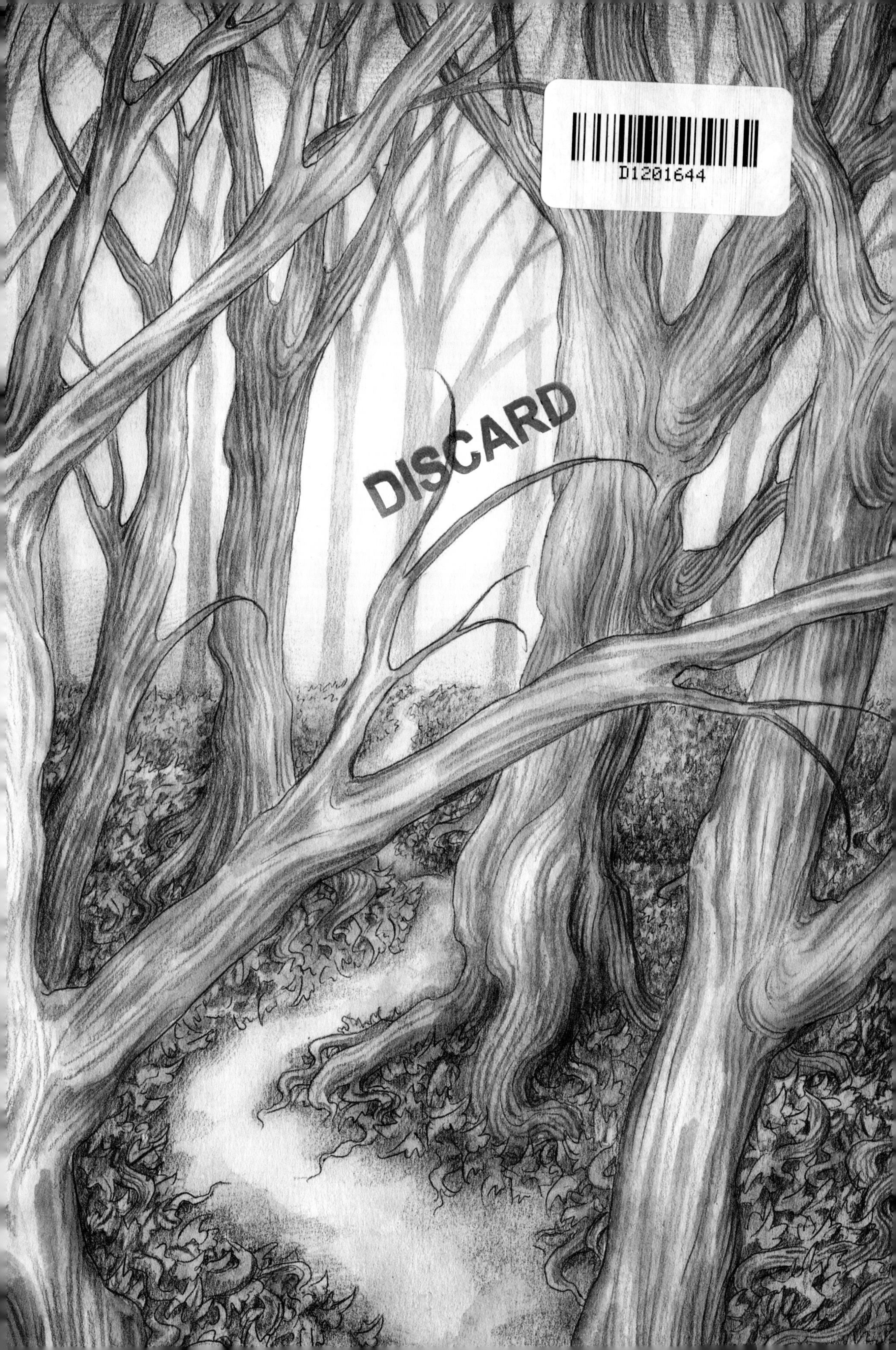

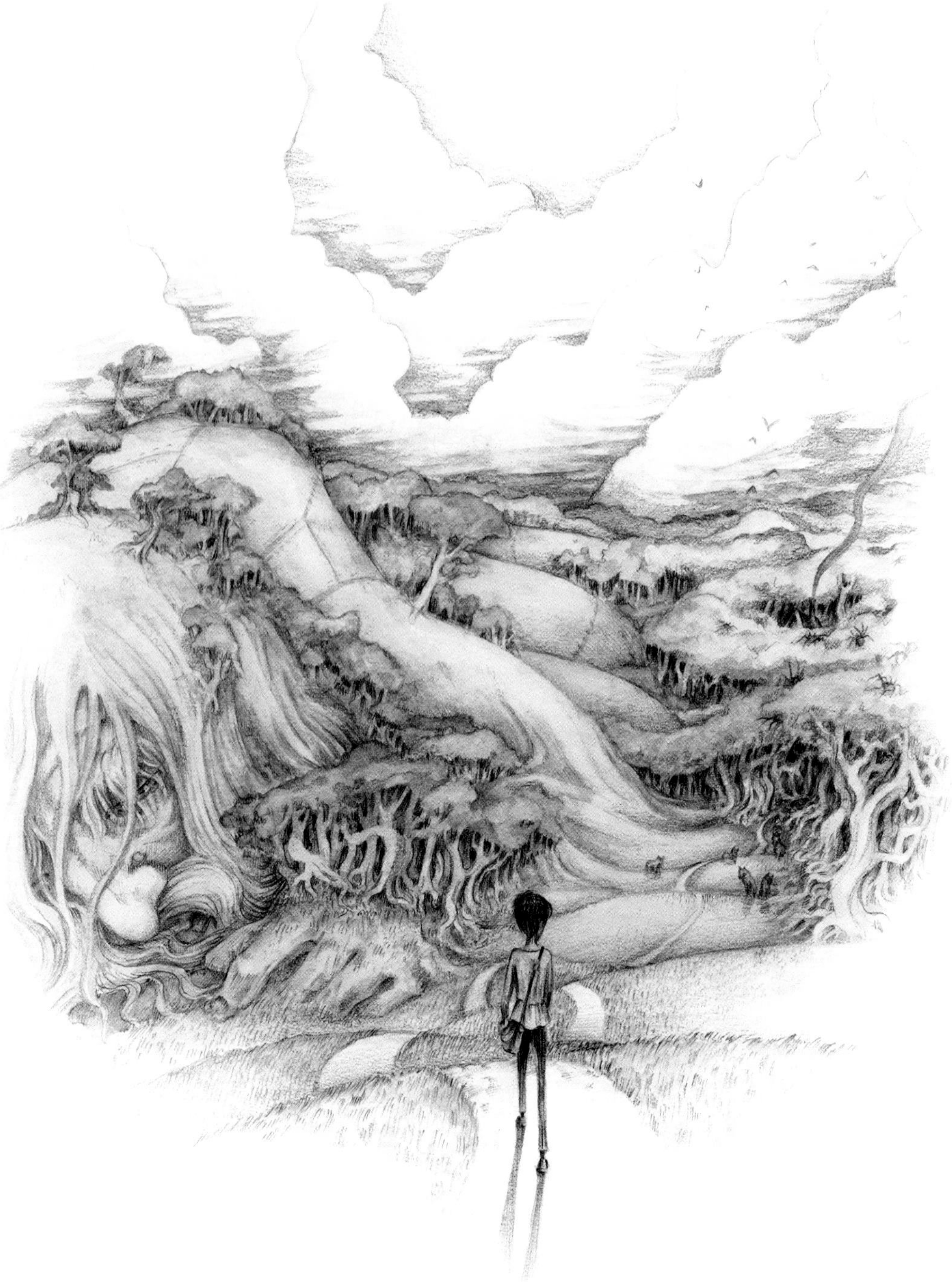

Leo LaFleur & Adam Oehlers

The
ERRAND

SIMPLY READ BOOKS

Published in 2017 by Simply Read Books
www.simplyreadbooks.com

Text © 2017 Leo LaFleur
Illustrations © 2017 Adam Oehlers

Library and Archives Canada Cataloguing in Publication
LaFleur, Leo, 1980–, author
The errand / written by Leo LaFleur ; illustrated by
Adam Oehlers.

ISBN 978-1-77229-024-0 (hardcover)

1. Graphic novels. 1. Oehlers, Adam, illustrator 11. Title.

PN6733.L34E77 2017   j741.5′971   C2017-902891-X

We gratefully acknowledge for their financial support of our publishing
program the Canada Council for the Arts, the BC Arts Council, and the
Government of Canada through the Canada Book Fund (CBF).

Manufactured in South Korea
Book design by Naomi MacDougall

10 9 8 7 6 5 4 3 2 1

This story is dedicated to my nephews:
Aaron, Ethan, Seth, and William;
my niece Madeline, and my godson Gabriel.
May your dreams in this world ever
guide your reality.
Leo

For Nom, Nova, and Vaida,
Kim Fiester, Vanessa Poling Savona,
Robin McIntosh, Emily Crooker,
and Bruce Priore, for your
incredible support.
Adam

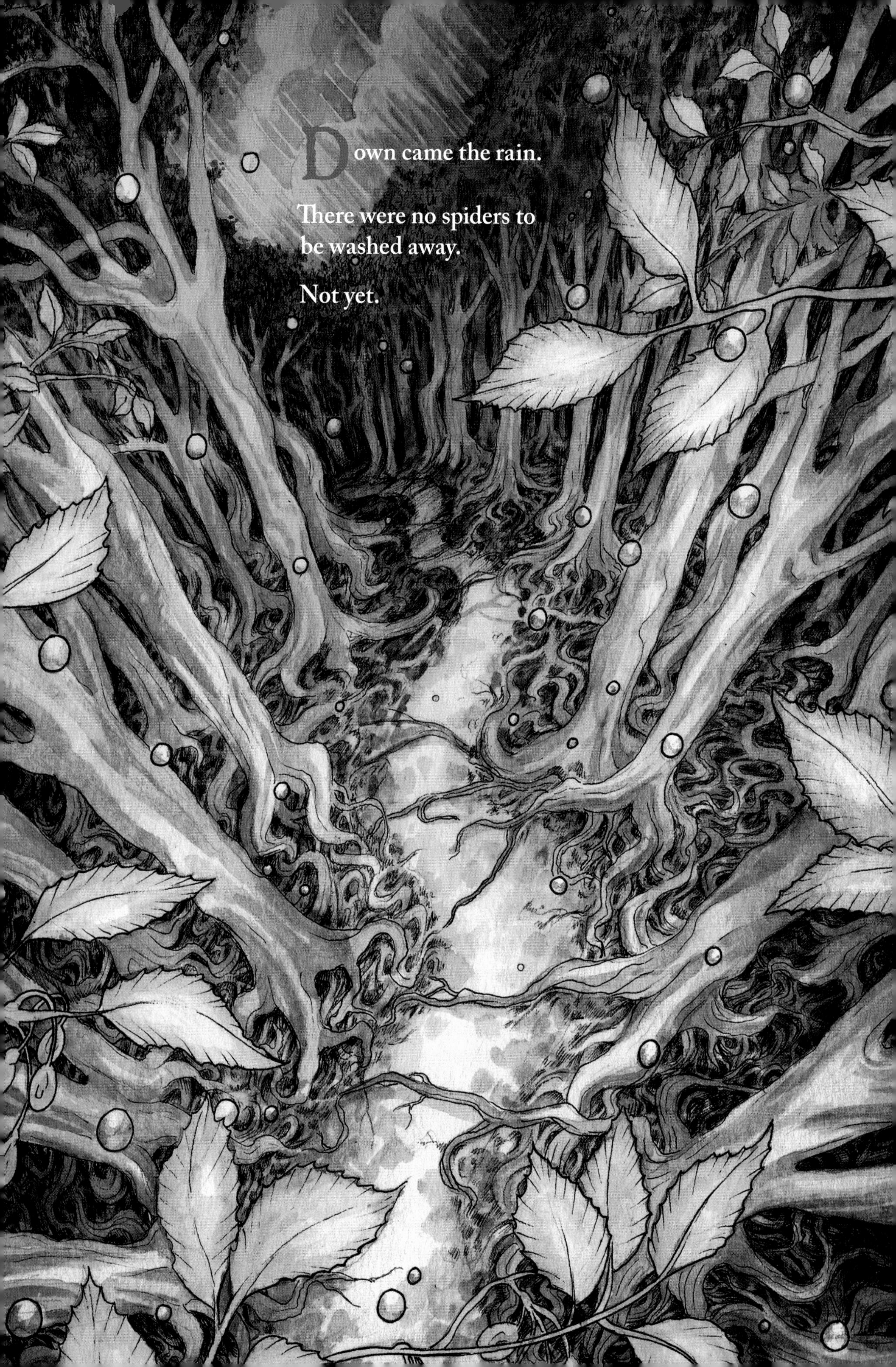

Down came the rain.

There were no spiders to be washed away.

Not yet.

The forest will hold water for you for a time, but you must hurry.

Soon the leaves will not save you, for the small pools they carry will swell too high and too wide, brimming over like tens of thousands of tiny waterfalls spluttering on and around you.

You must hurry.

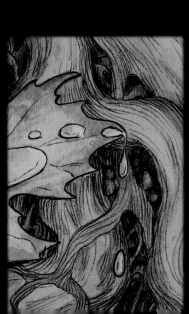

You must stay dry at all costs.

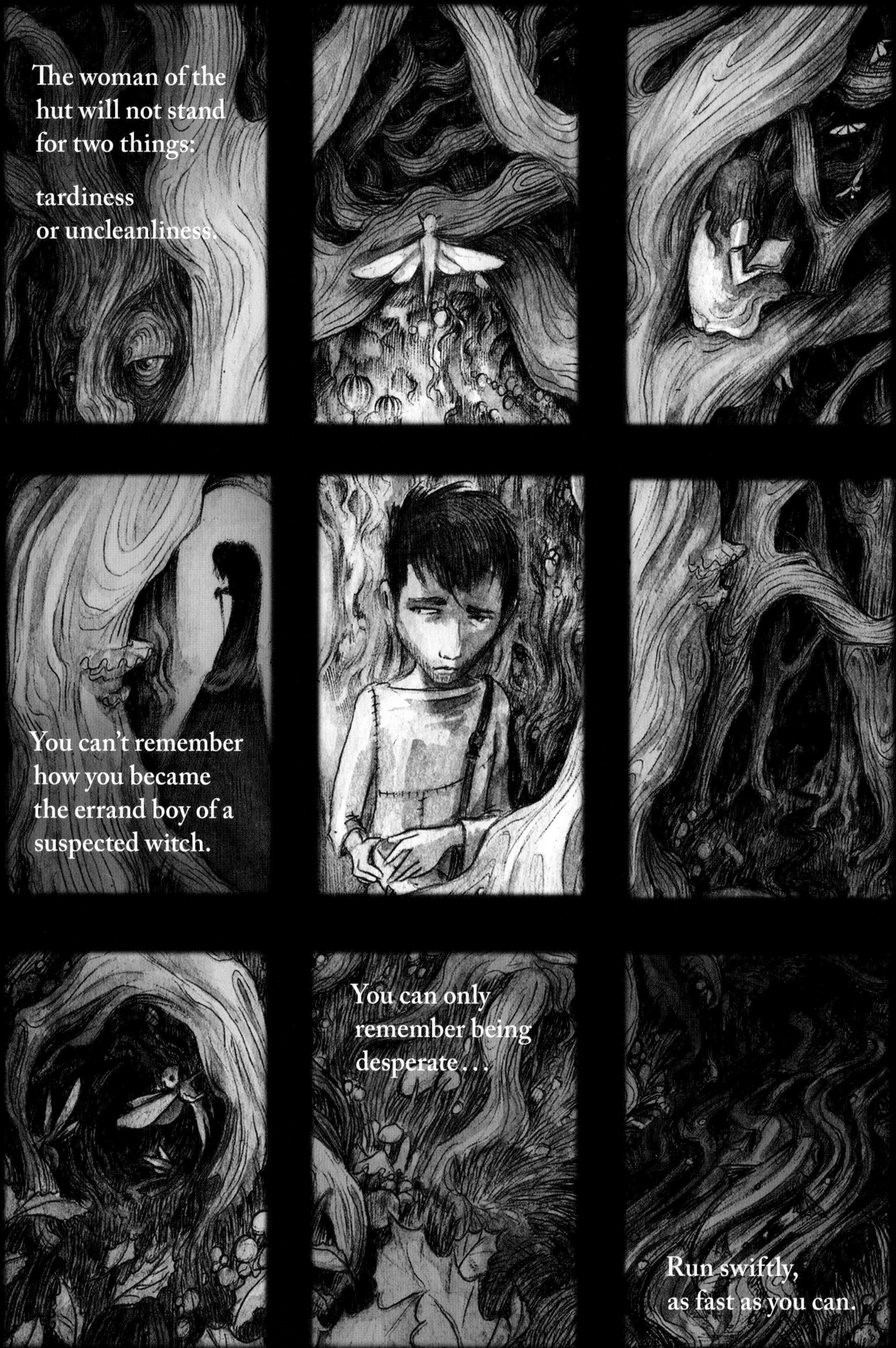
The woman of the hut will not stand for two things:
tardiness or uncleanliness.
You can't remember how you became the errand boy of a suspected witch.
You can only remember being desperate . . .
Run swiftly, as fast as you can.

There are other dangers here.
You know this.

To reach the witch's hut, one must beware of all
those creatures of the Whispering Woods.

The day is breaking,
The rain is shaking the leaves on the trees.

A drop here,

a drop there,

move faster,

pick up speed.

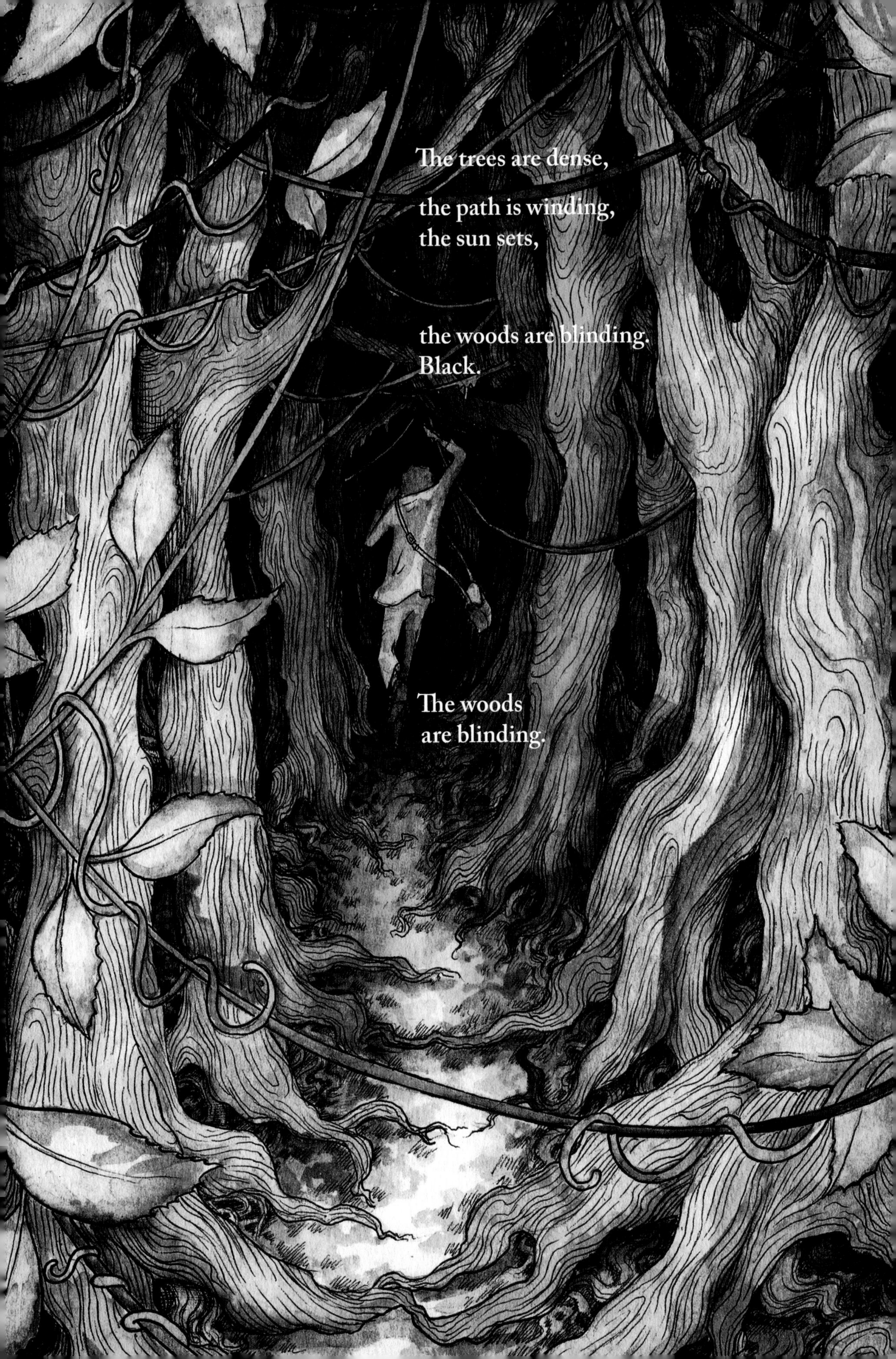

The trees are dense,

the path is winding,
the sun sets,

the woods are blinding.
Black.

The woods
are blinding.

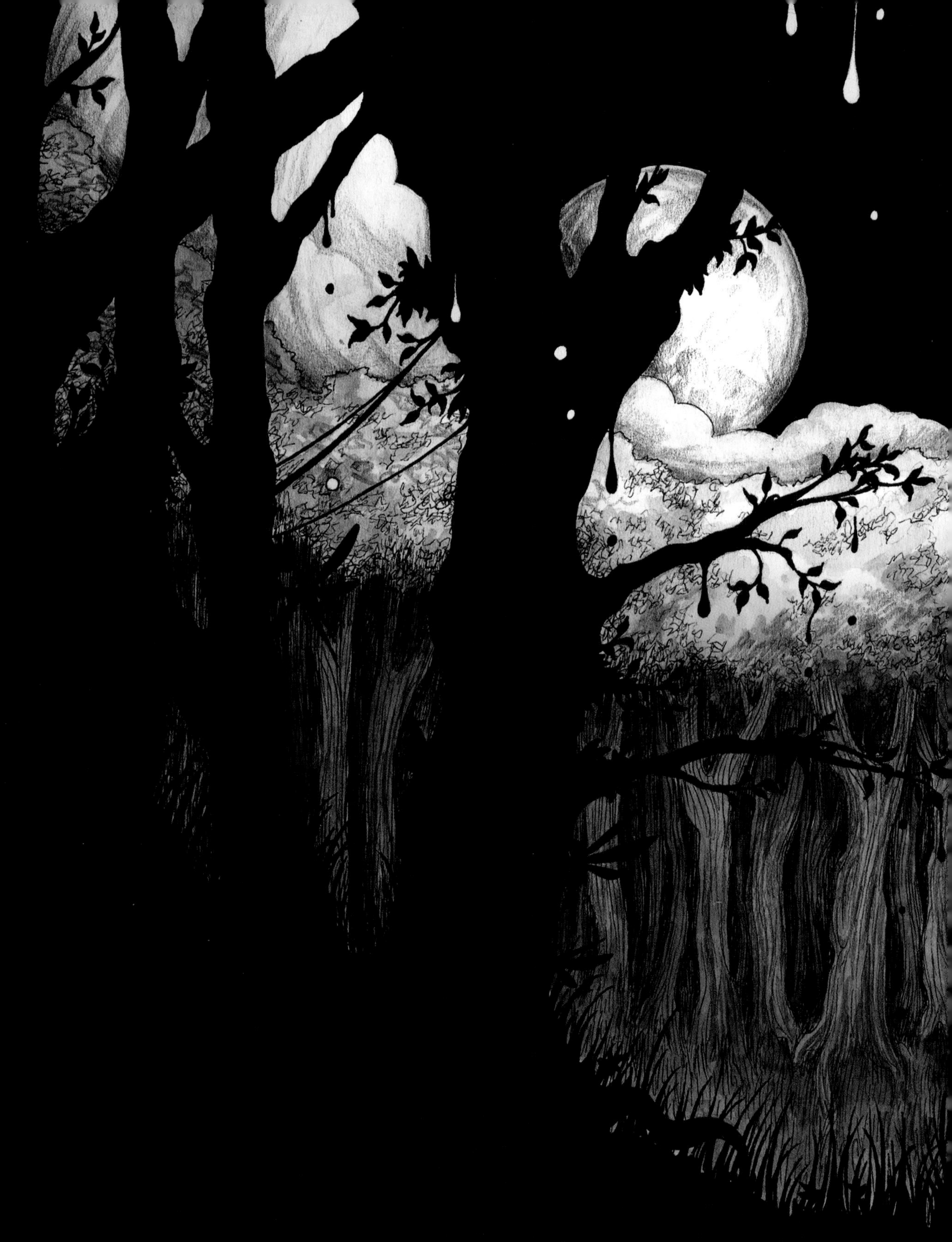

The rain stops.

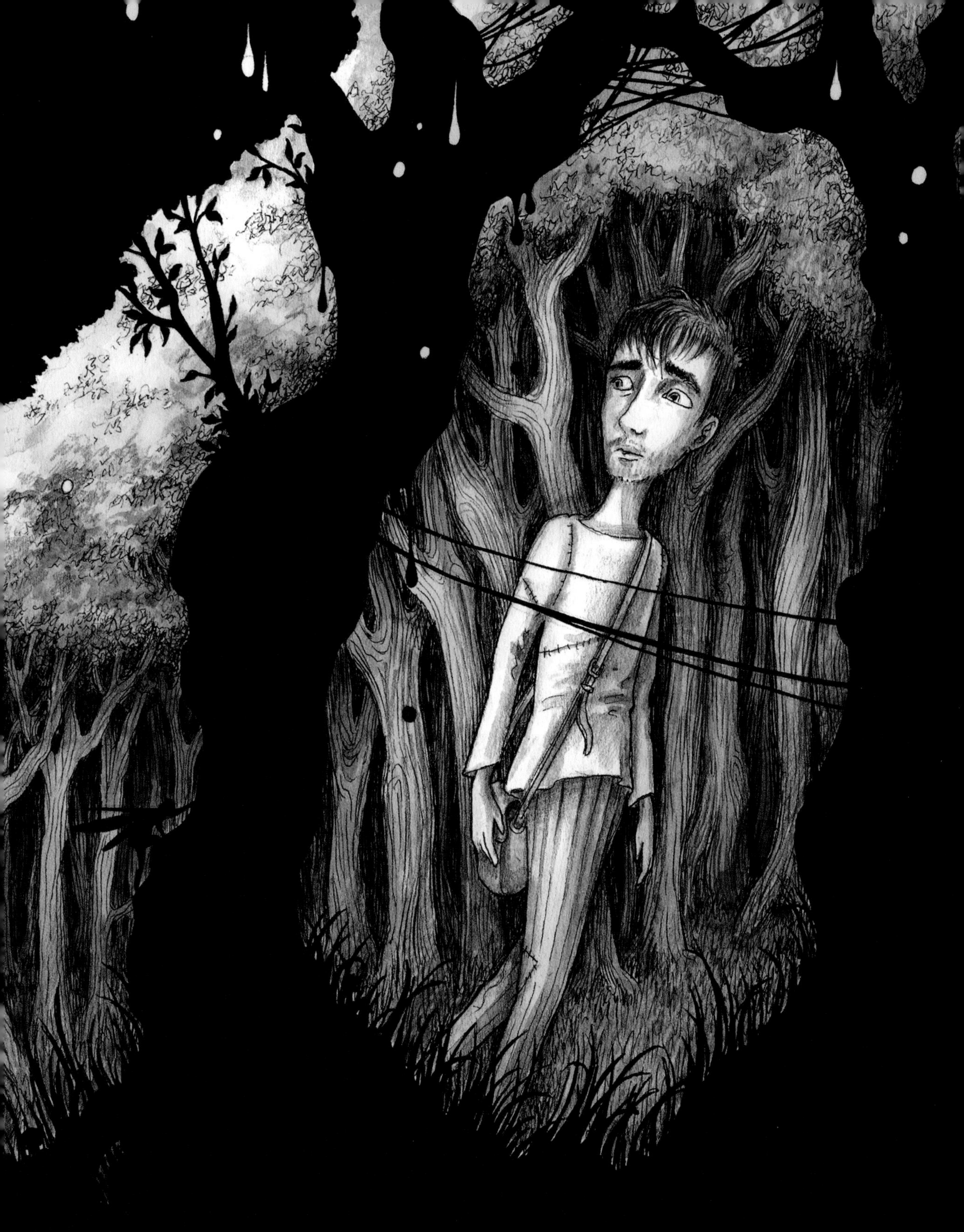

You slow to a walk with a deep sigh.

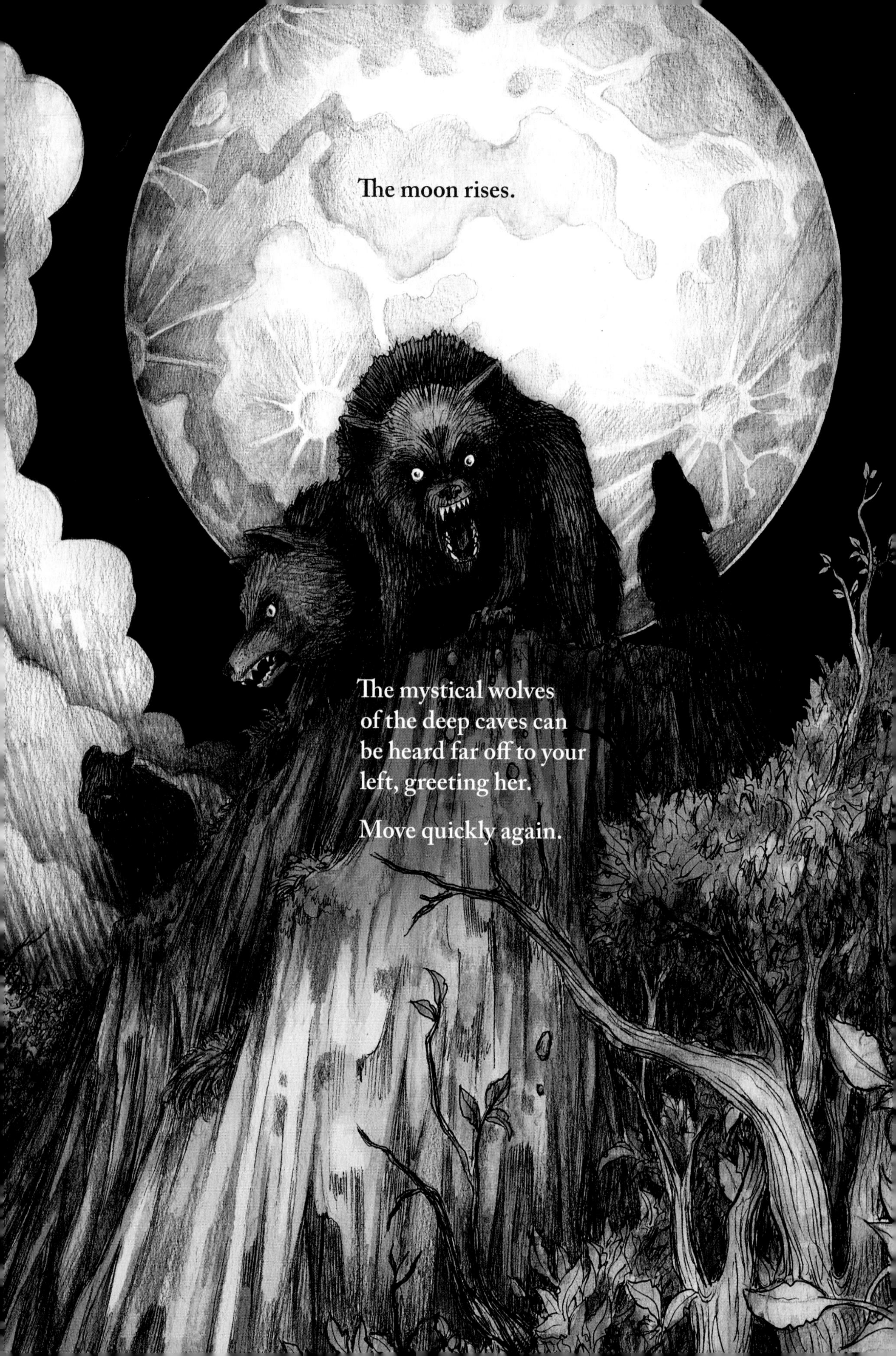
The moon rises.
The mystical wolves of the deep caves can be heard far off to your left, greeting her.
Move quickly again.

Remember the spiders?

None were washed out.
They all survived.

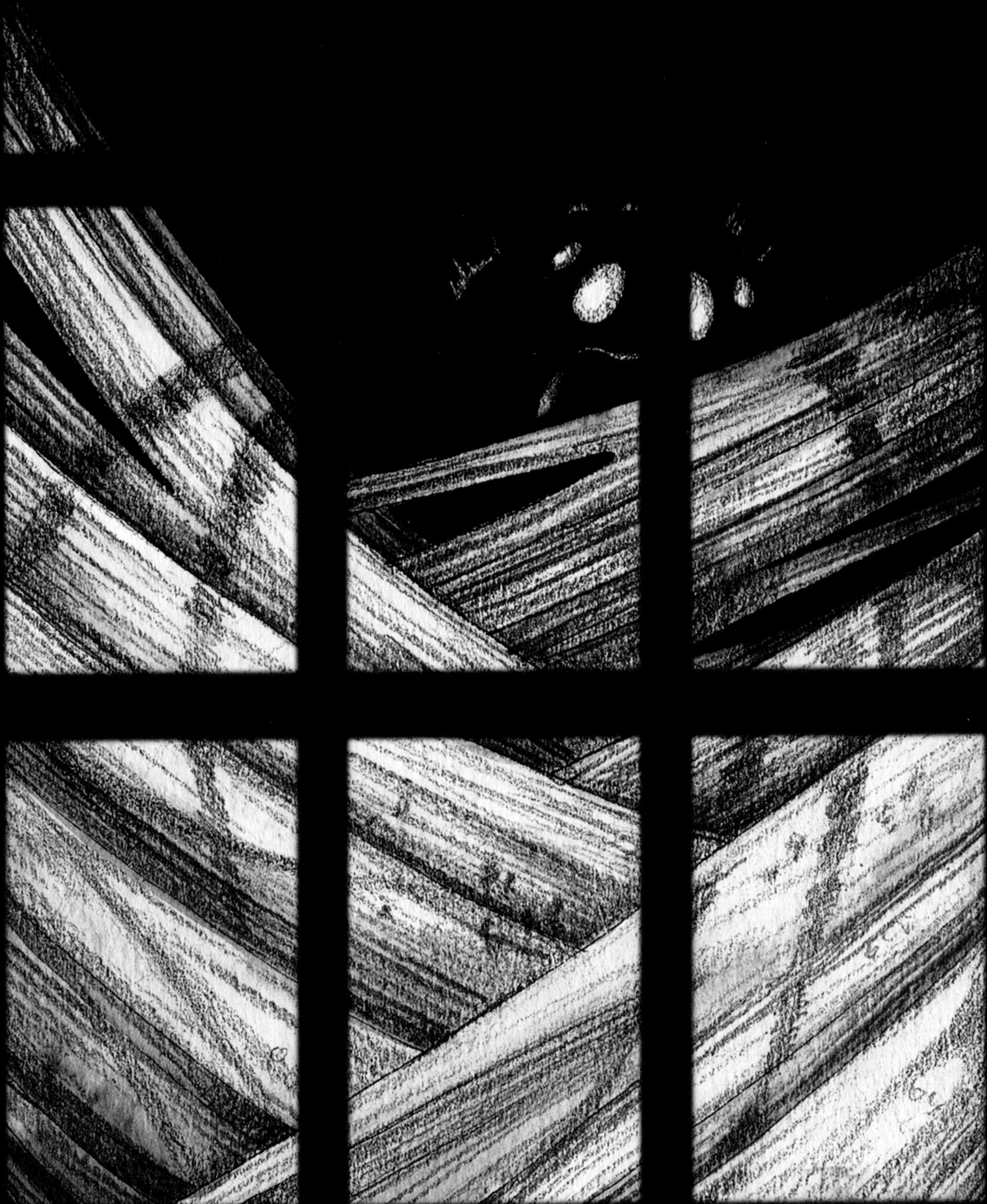

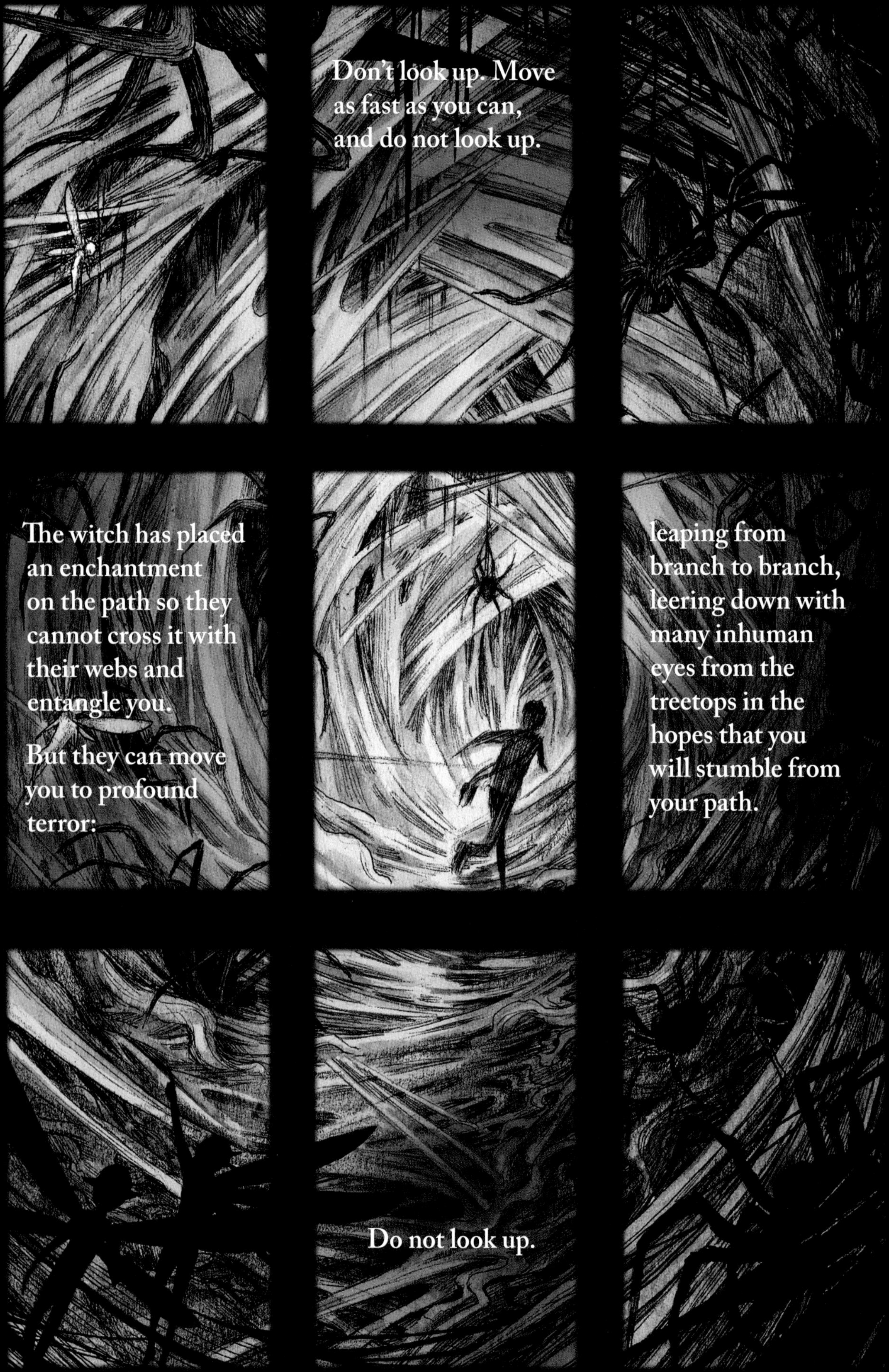
Don't look up. Move as fast as you can, and do not look up.
The witch has placed an enchantment on the path so they cannot cross it with their webs and entangle you.
But they can move you to profound terror:
leaping from branch to branch, leering down with many inhuman eyes from the treetops in the hopes that you will stumble from your path.
Do not look up.

Not all things in the
woods are dark.

But most things in the
witch's Whispering Woods
are dark.

Some things have
crept back with
new hope.

Beings not of darkness,

but of light.

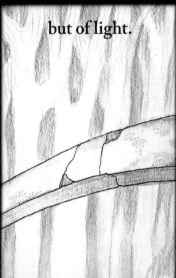

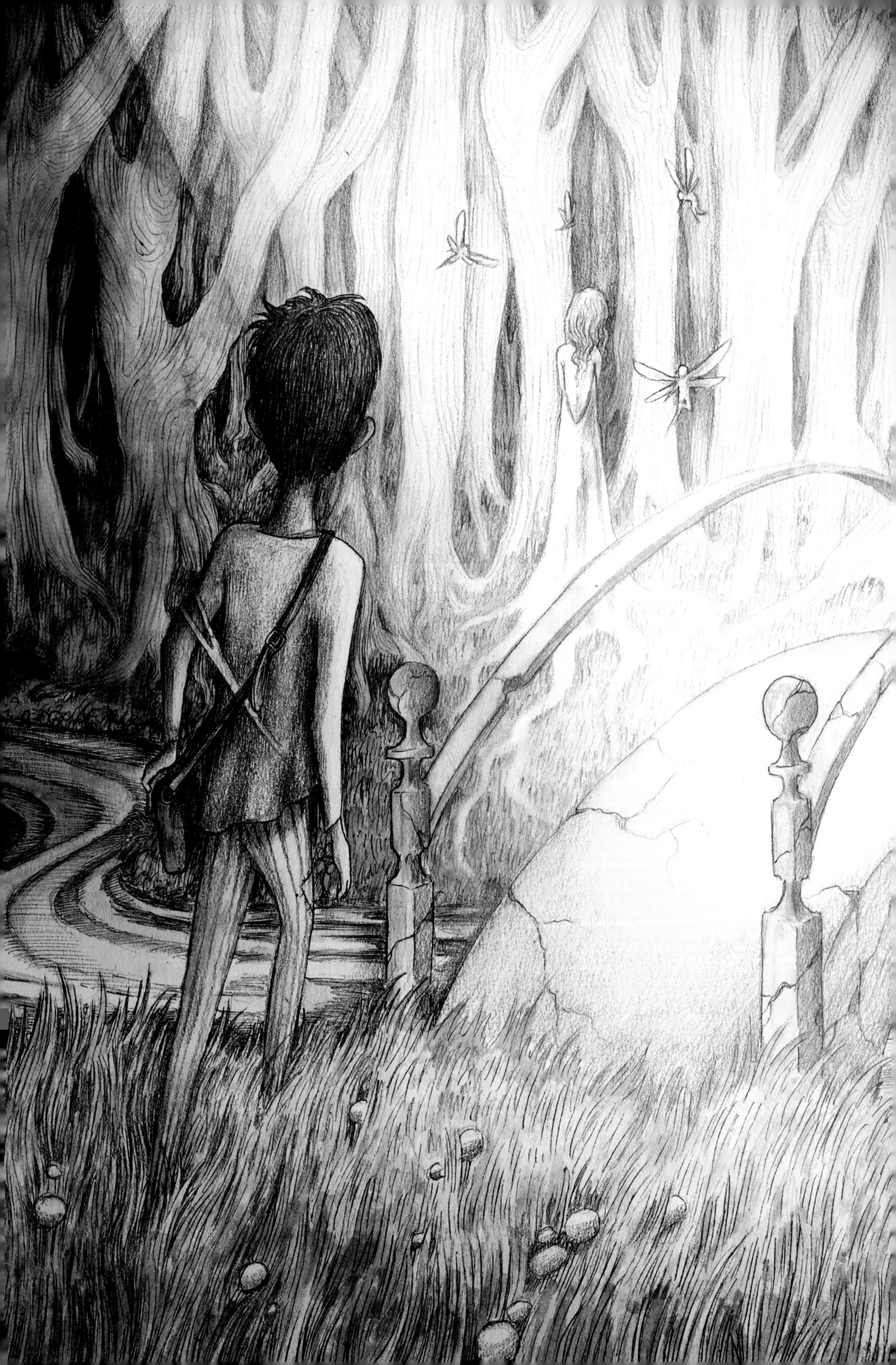

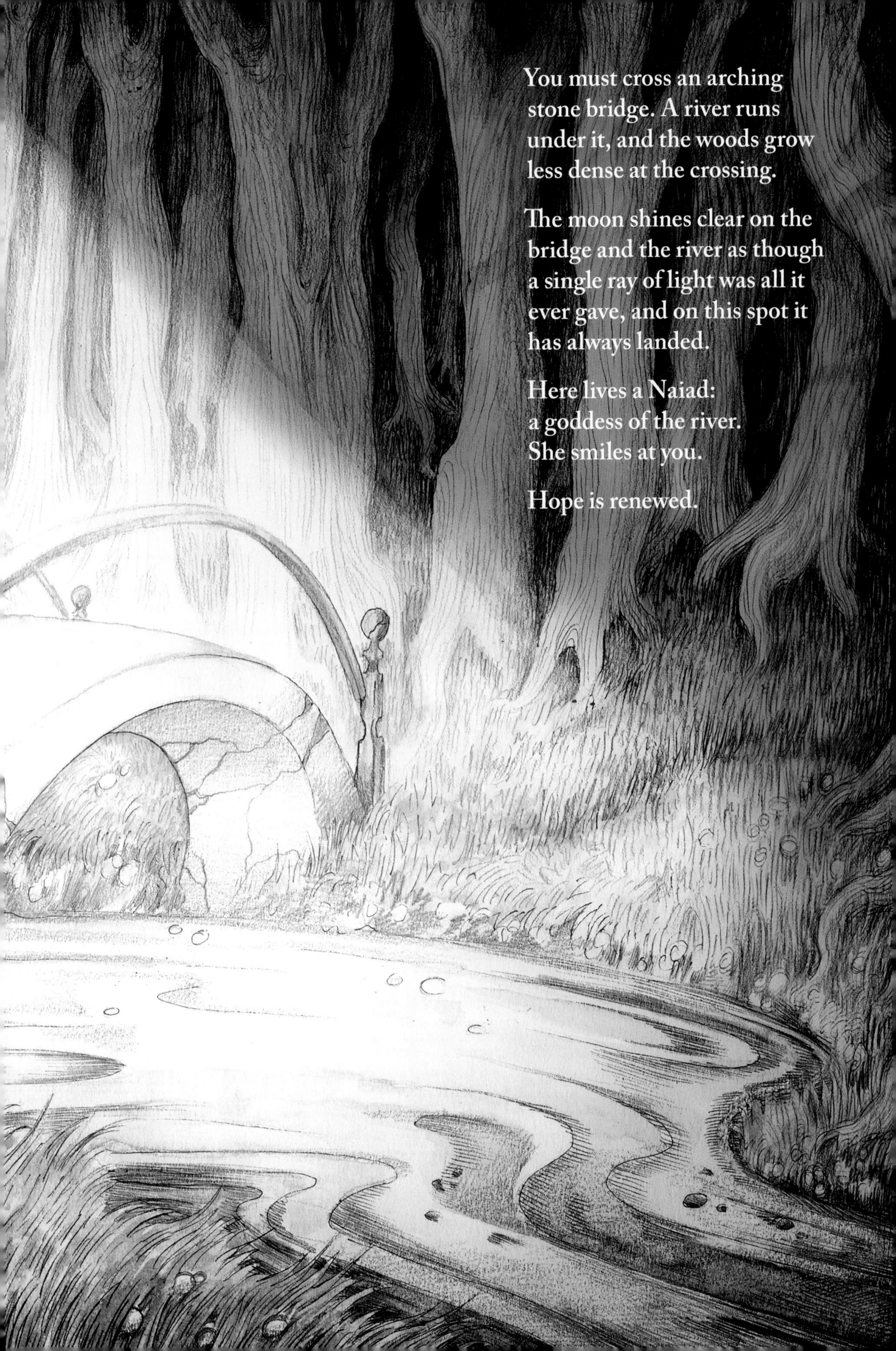

You must cross an arching stone bridge. A river runs under it, and the woods grow less dense at the crossing.

The moon shines clear on the bridge and the river as though a single ray of light was all it ever gave, and on this spot it has always landed.

Here lives a Naiad:
a goddess of the river.
She smiles at you.

Hope is renewed.

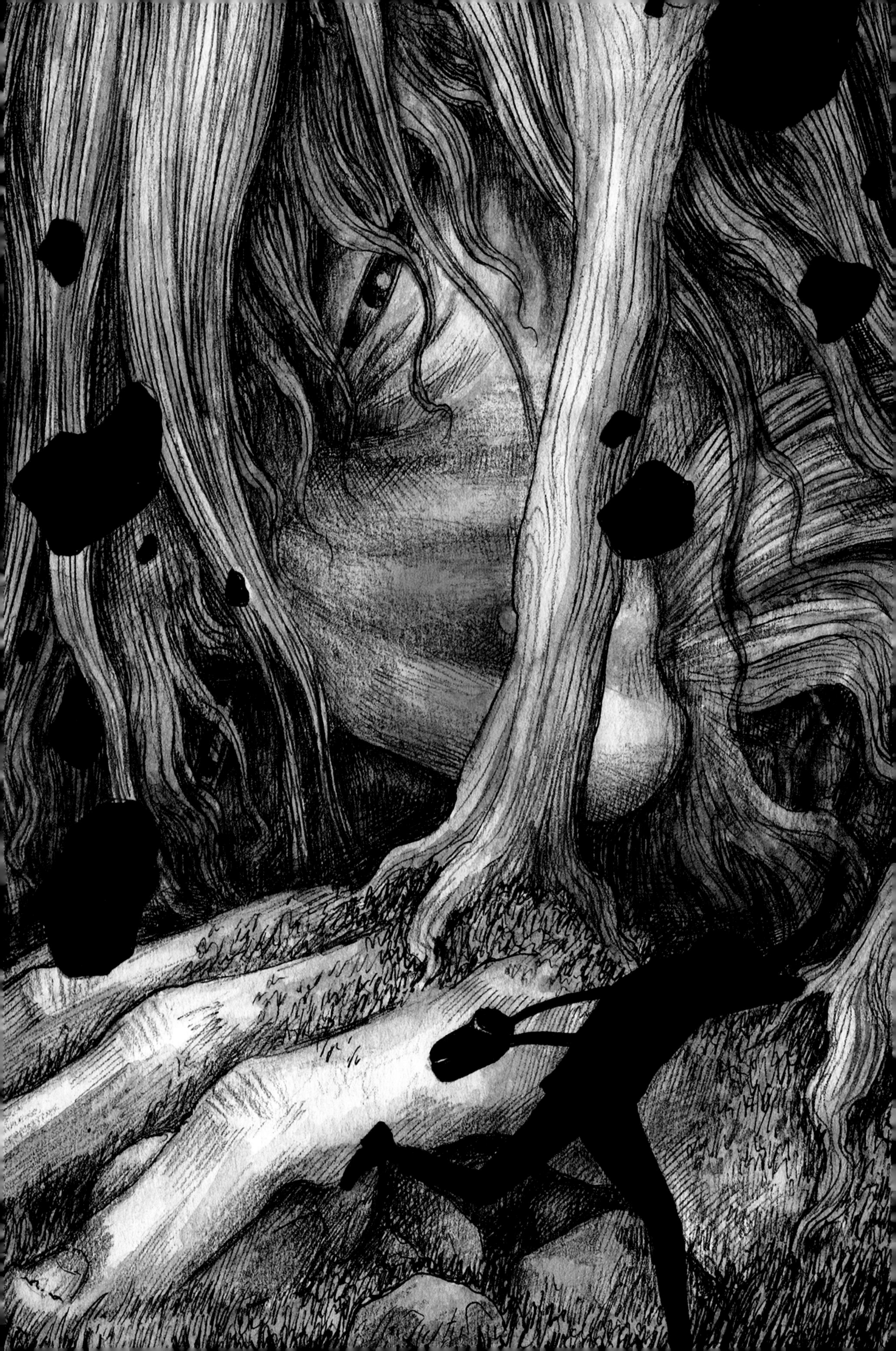

You can hear it.
The rumble.
You can feel it. The shaking.

But you do not fear the giant's
snoring, for the glow of the
Naiad's smile is upon you.
Still, you do not slow your pace.
The giant, in one hand,
could hold seven of you.

He will wake within the hour.

Finally you can see the
unholy smoke of the witch's
simmering broil rising from
her hut on the other
side of a valley.

It is not a warm view, like
seeing your home as a
miniature in the distance,
but it is better than the
woods at night . . .

or so you think.

Lately you've felt strange there. You can't be sure she's a witch, but you no longer doubt it either.

How did you find yourself as the errand boy of the witch of the Whispering Woods?

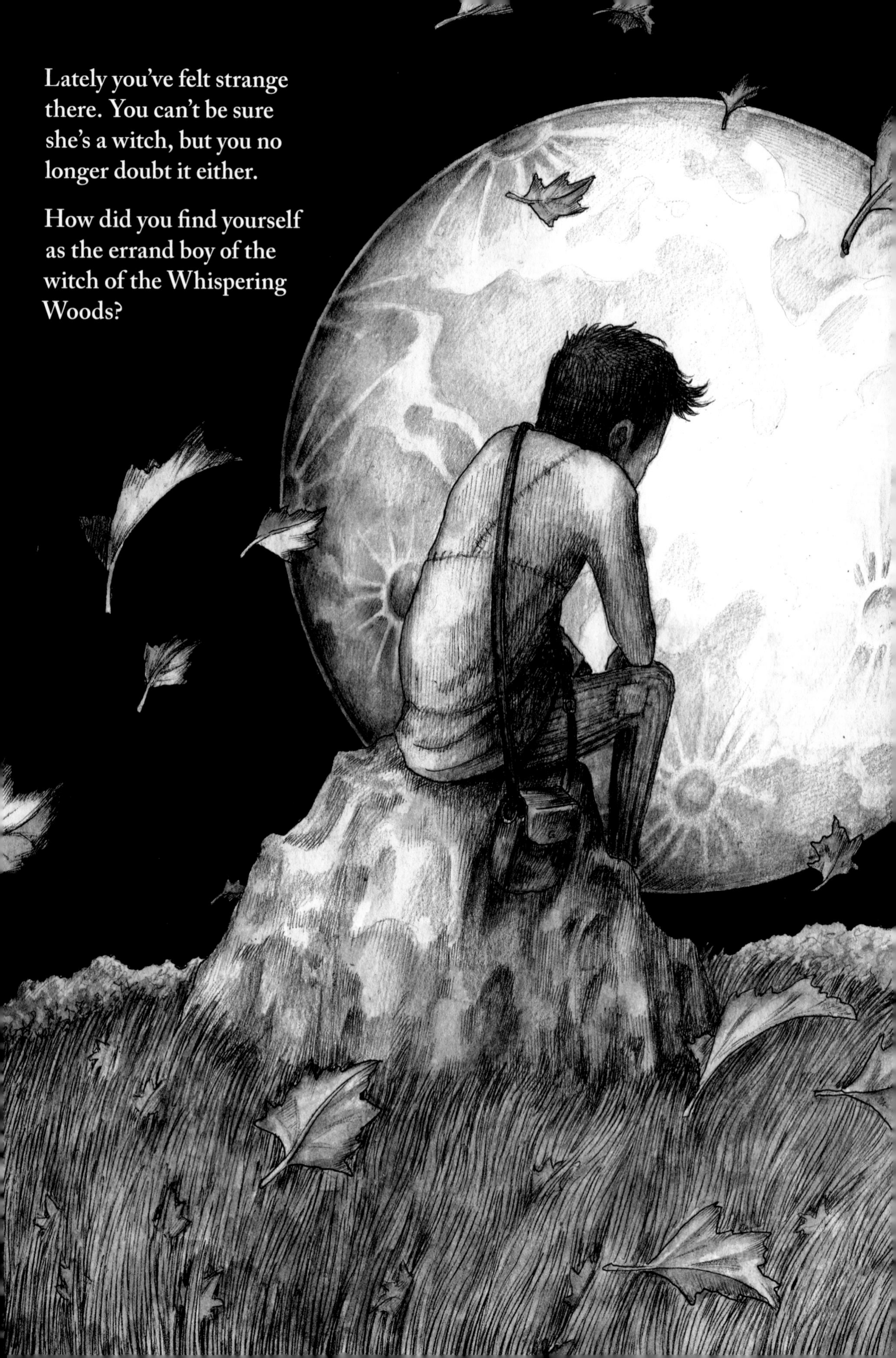

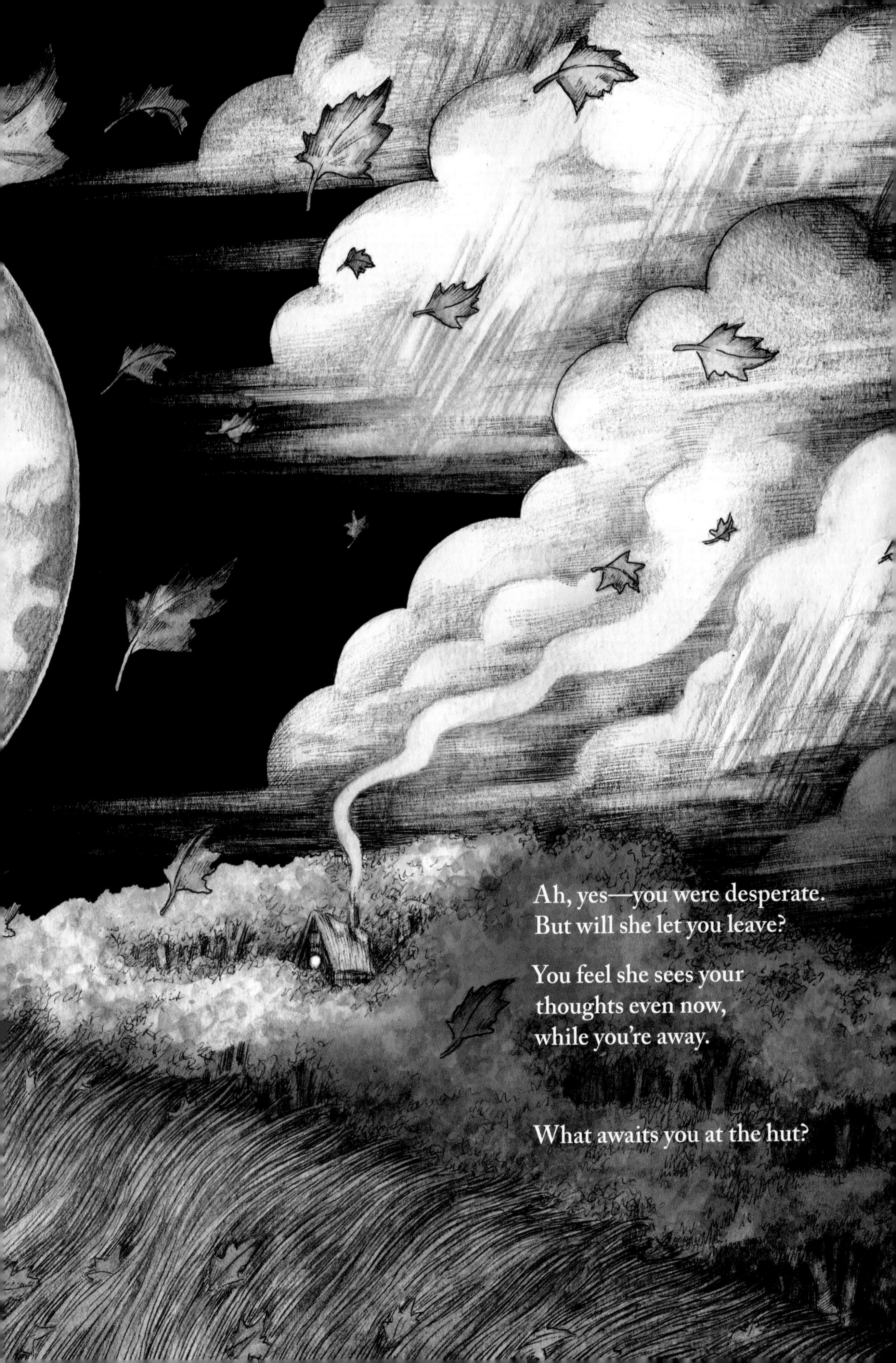

Ah, yes—you were desperate.
But will she let you leave?

You feel she sees your
thoughts even now,
while you're away.

What awaits you at the hut?

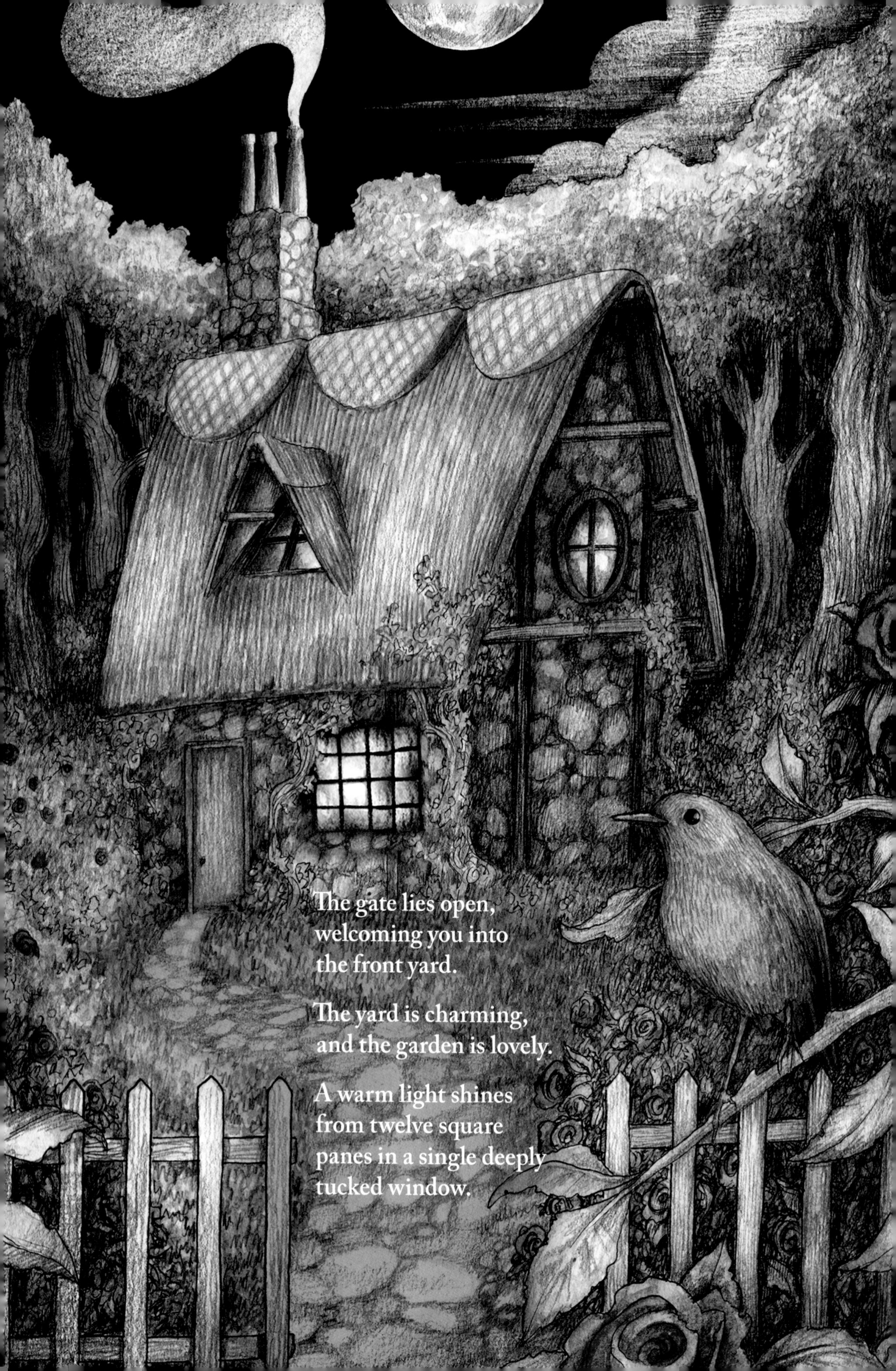

The gate lies open, welcoming you into the front yard.

The yard is charming, and the garden is lovely.

A warm light shines from twelve square panes in a single deeply tucked window.

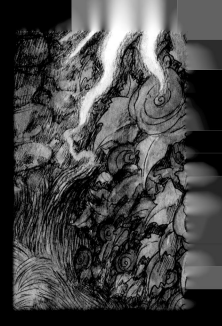

You walk down the path towards the small wooden door. The path, the yard, the garden, and the house are perfect.

Too perfect.

Magically perfect.

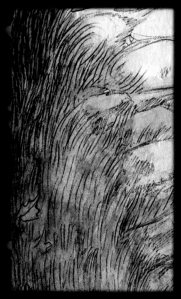

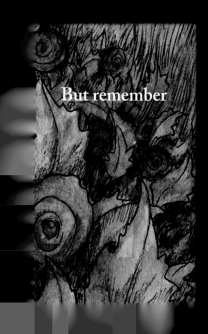

But remember

there is light

and new hope.

From the shadows of the roof, out steps a spirit of the wood, dressed in a flowing gown of liquid moonlight. She floats to you from the roof, shrinking all the while to the size of your heart.

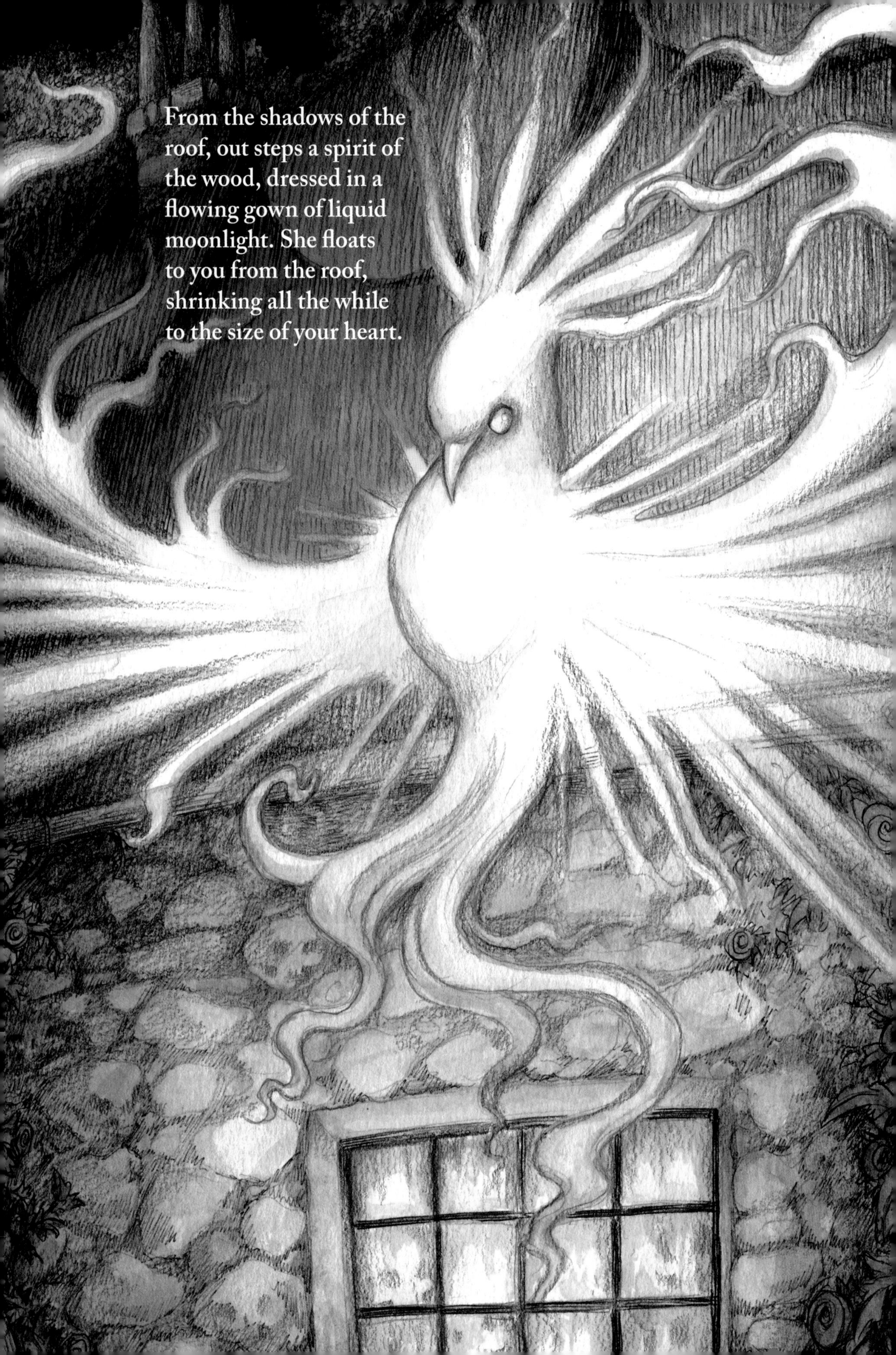

You open the door of your heart and let her in.
Your courage is unmistakable now.

But should something go awry, can a witch be
beaten with naught but courage?

Slowly, you turn the knob and open the door.

The warm light finds the night ever more,
as you find the inside of the hut.

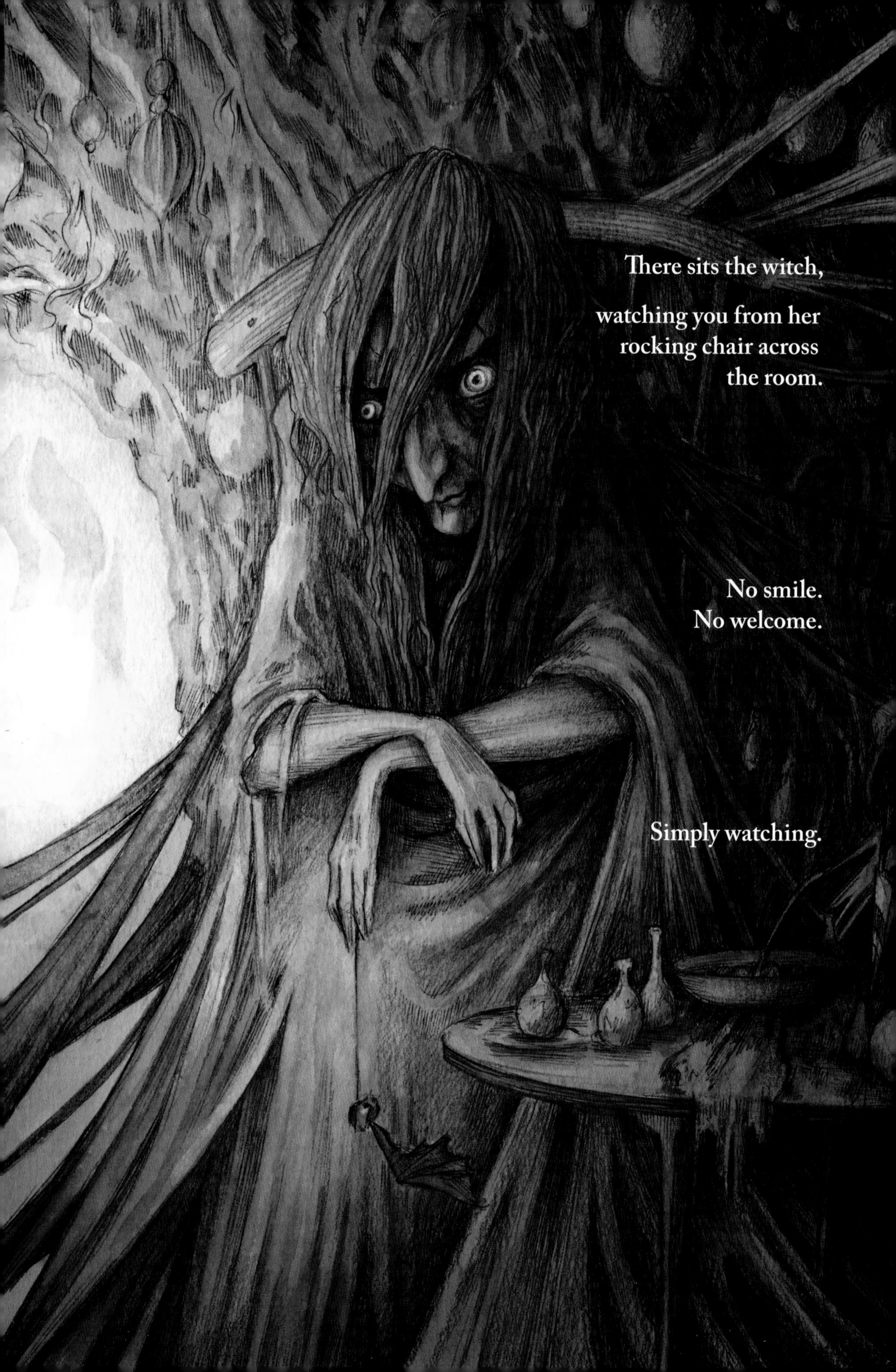

There sits the witch,

watching you from her
rocking chair across
the room.

No smile.
No welcome.

Simply watching.

She extends her very old
hands in search of the parcel.

You make your way slowly
towards her.

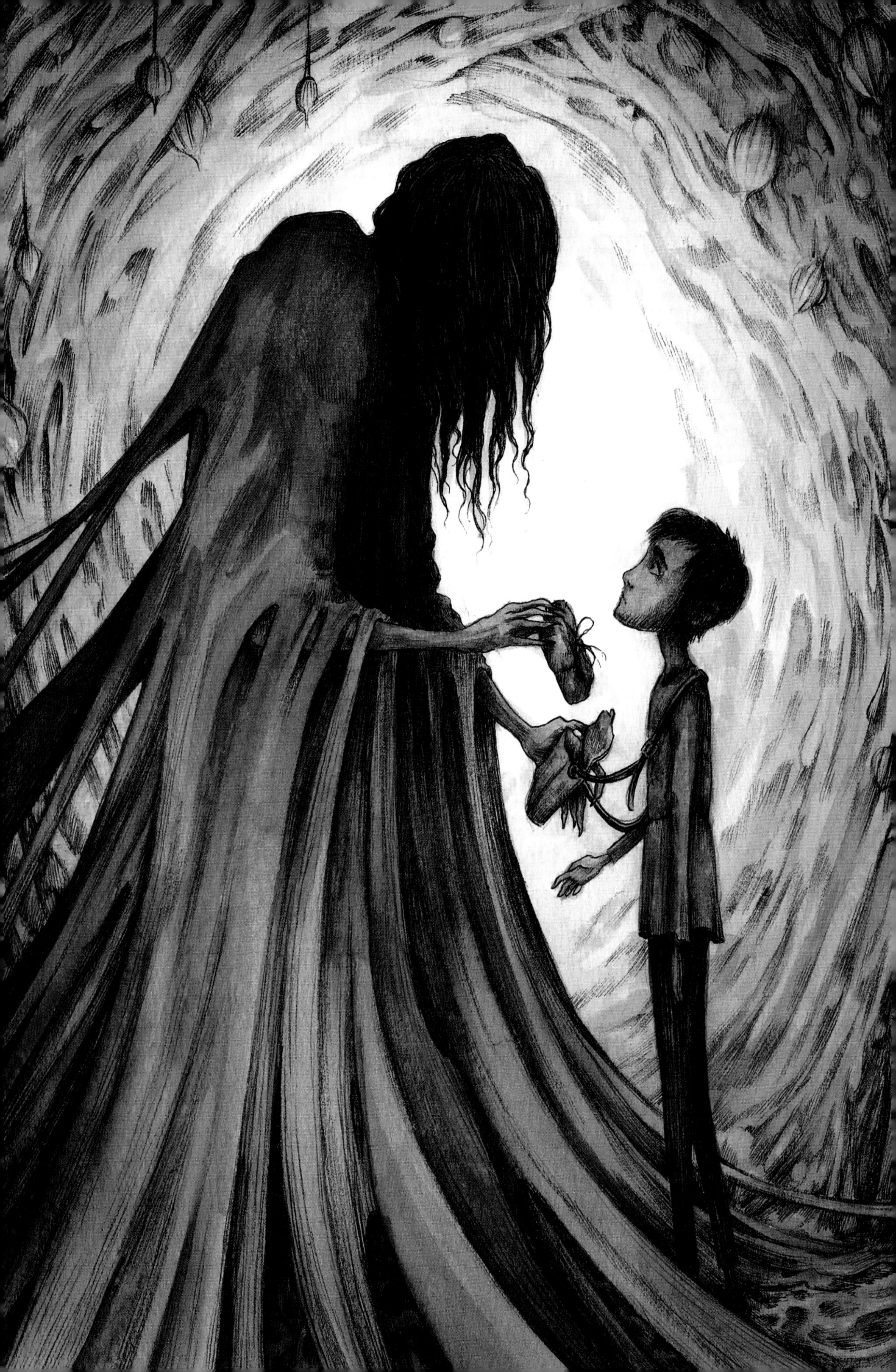

She snatches the parcel
from your hands,
but does not remove
her knowing glare.

It feels like you can't turn away.
As though weighty sand has replaced
the blood flow in your body.

Possibly an enchantment.

You test your new courage
and turn to leave.

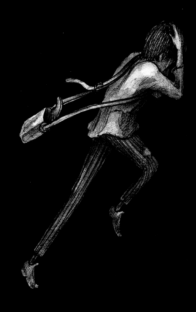

Quickly you run from
the witch's hut,

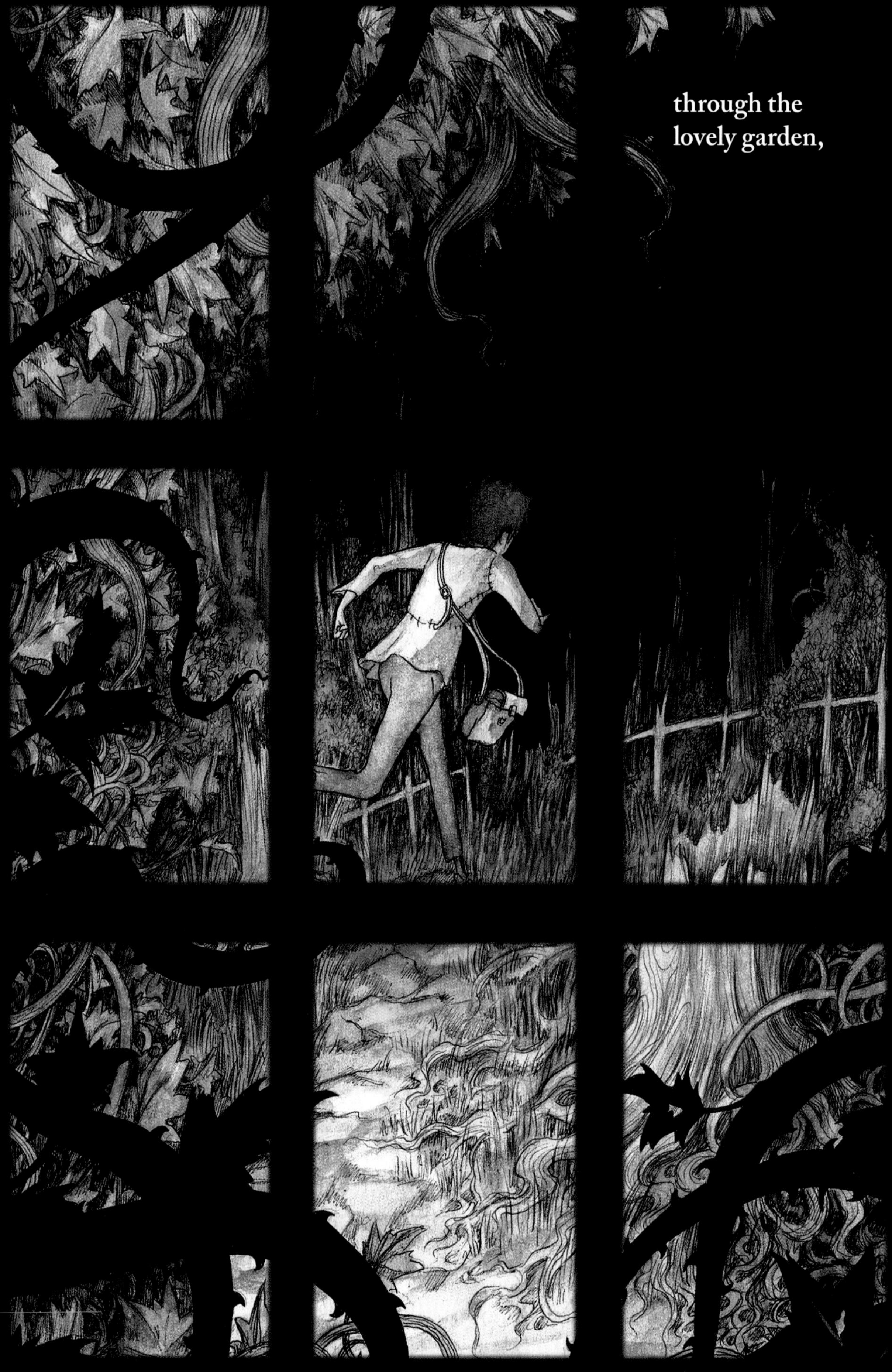

through the
lovely garden,

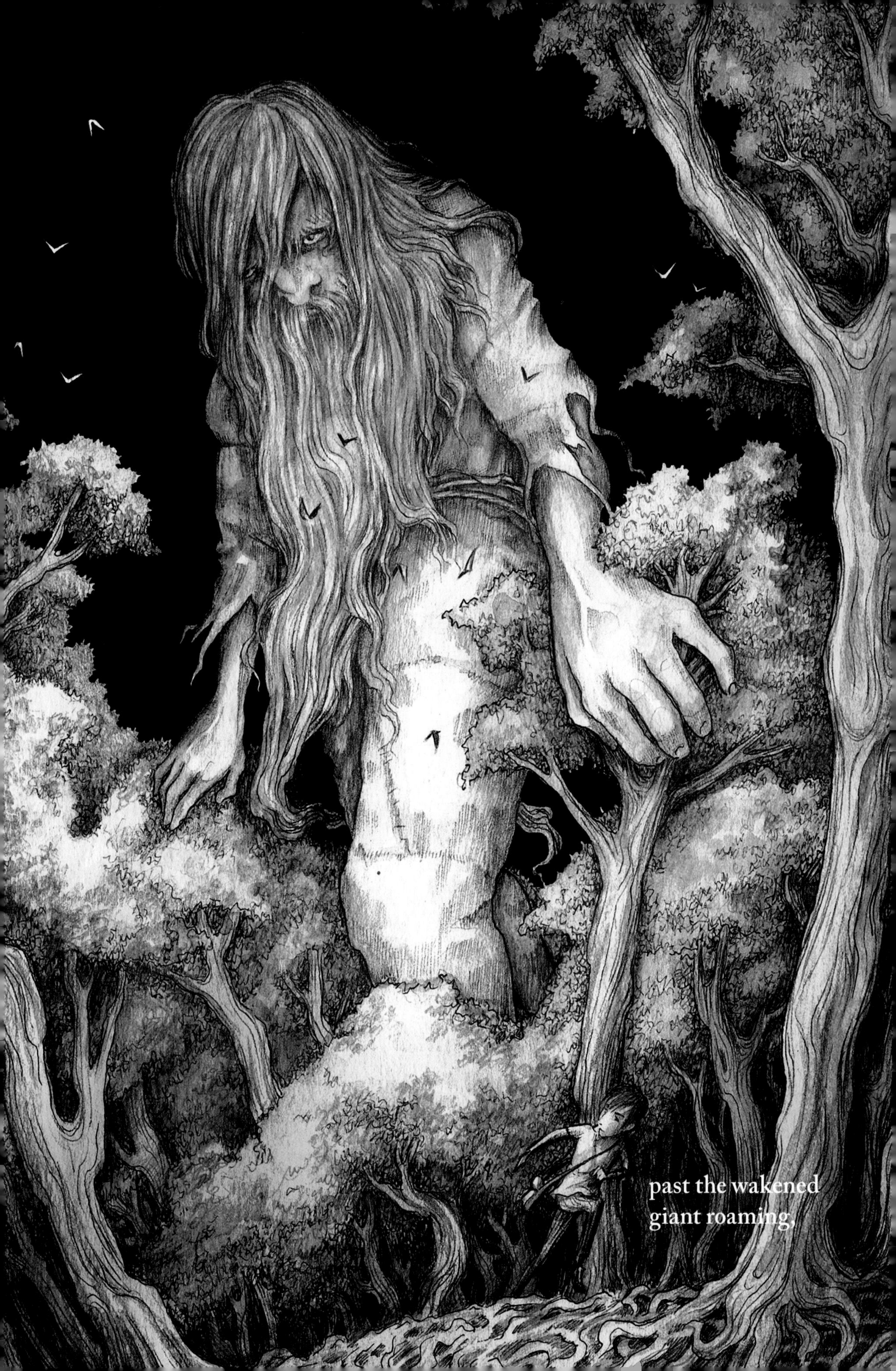

past the wakened
giant roaming,

over the bridge and
the moonlit river,

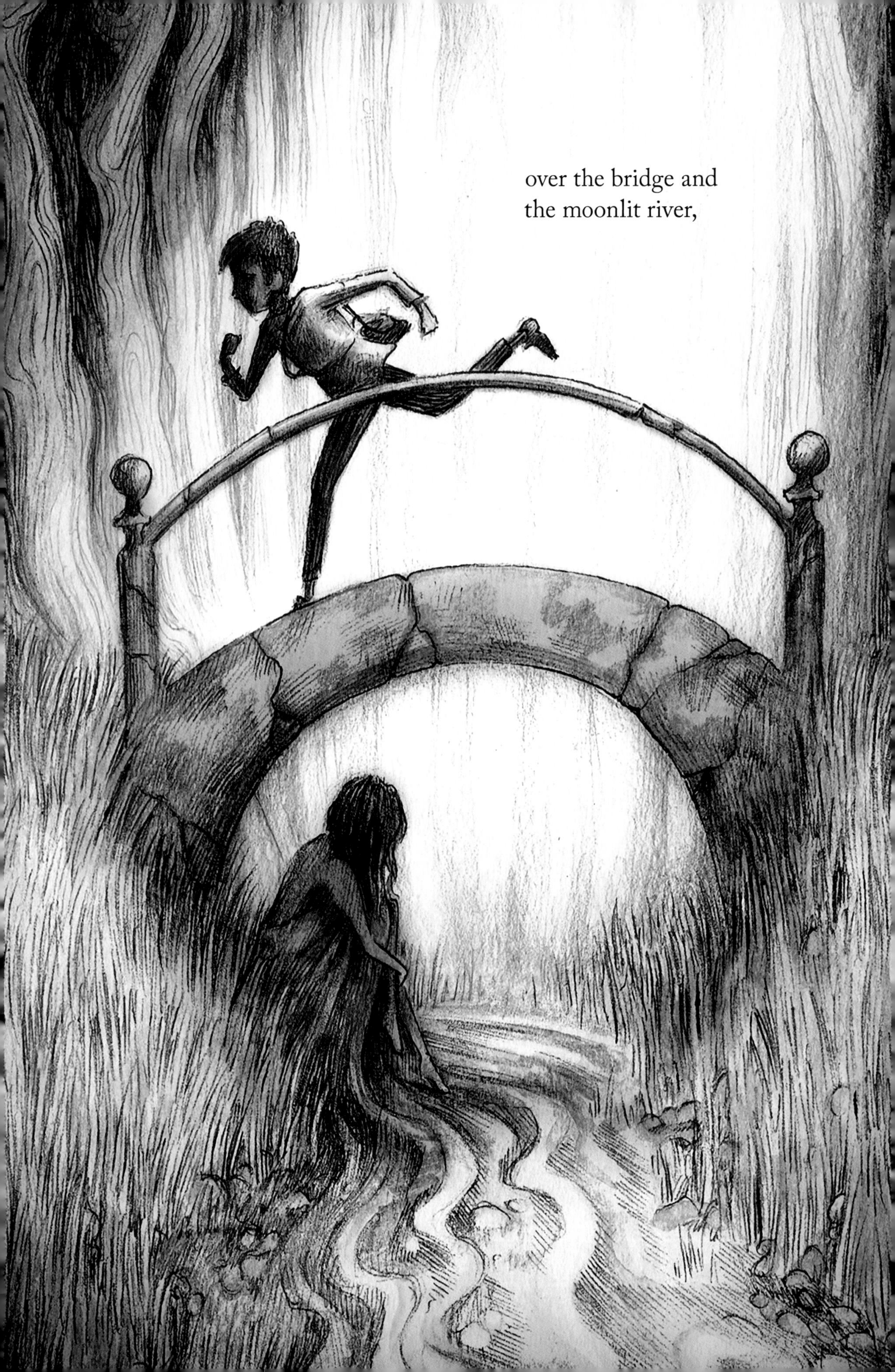

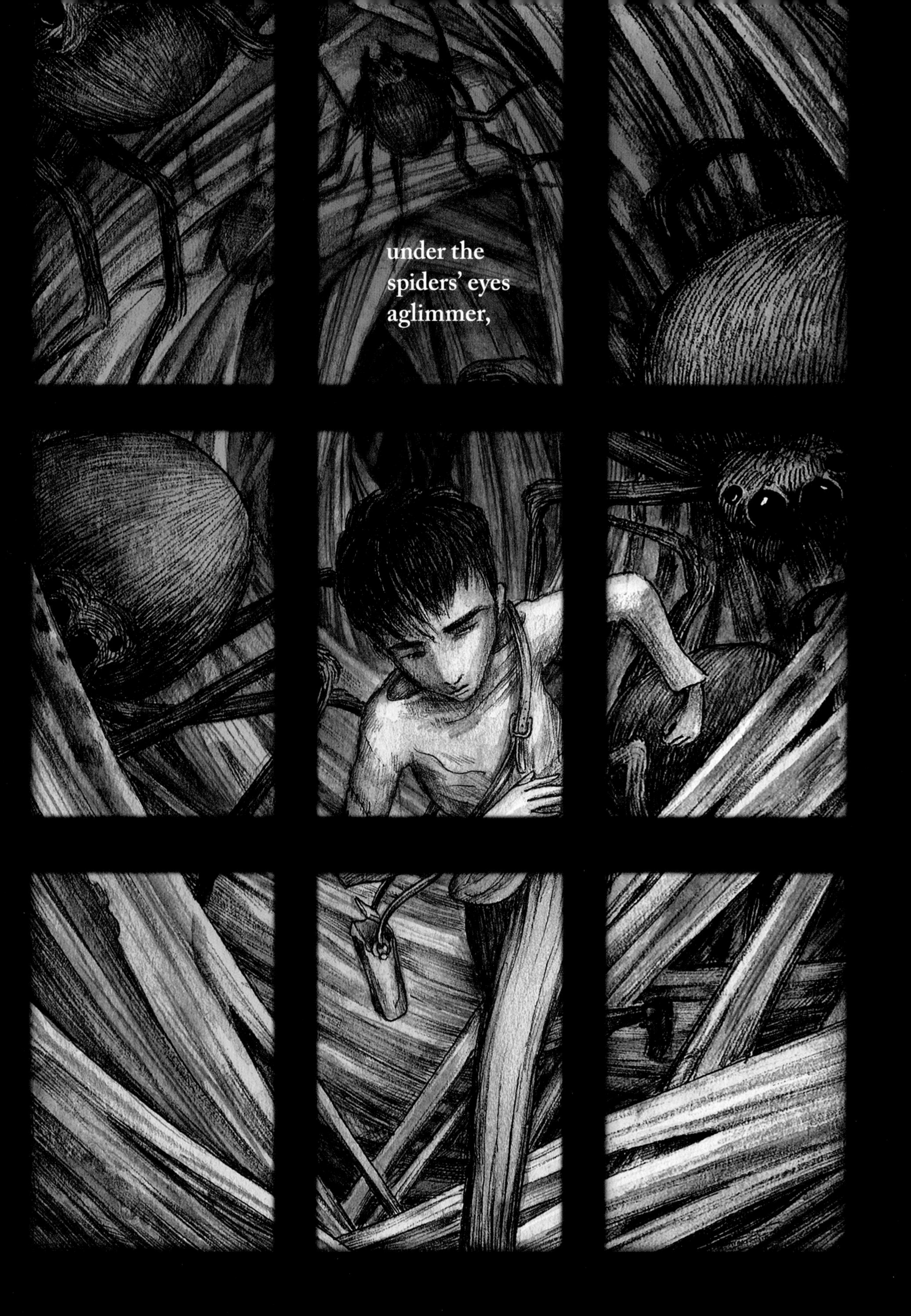
under the
spiders' eyes
aglimmer,

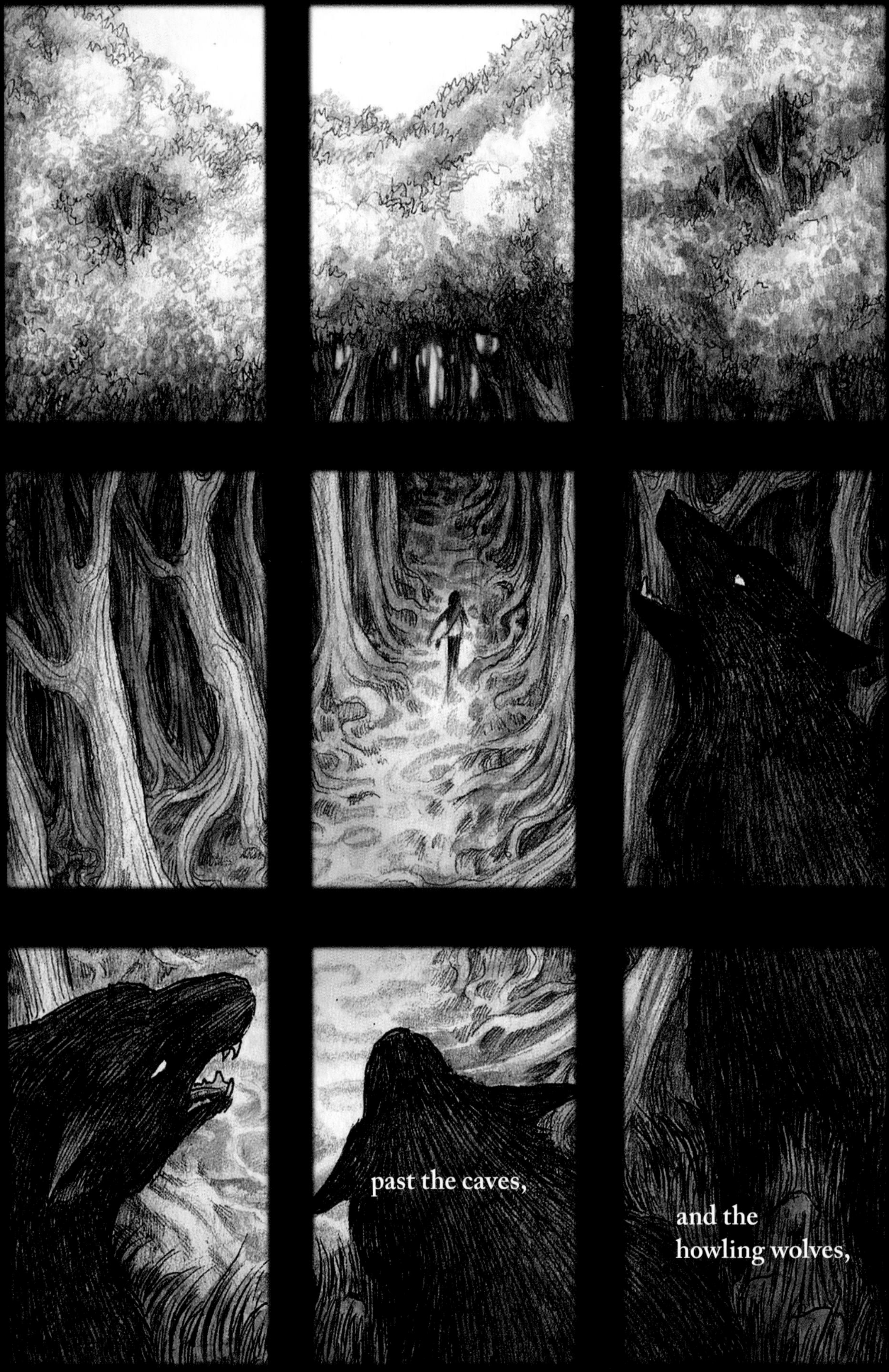
past the caves,
and the
howling wolves,

finding your feet on the path
just outside the witch's Whispering
Woods – a simple errand boy again,
who has had enough adventure
for this night with the
dreams of magic.

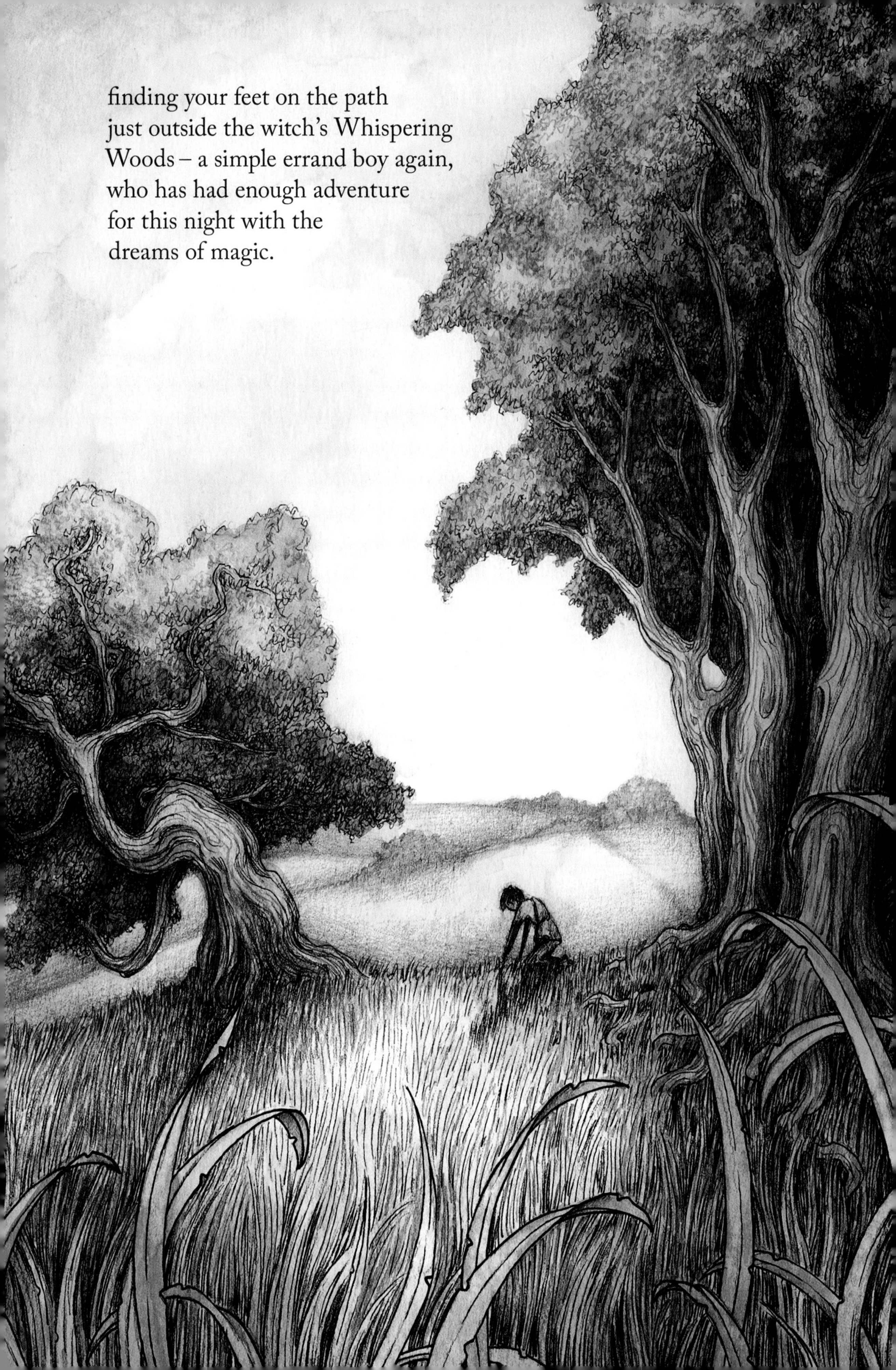

Until tomorrow...

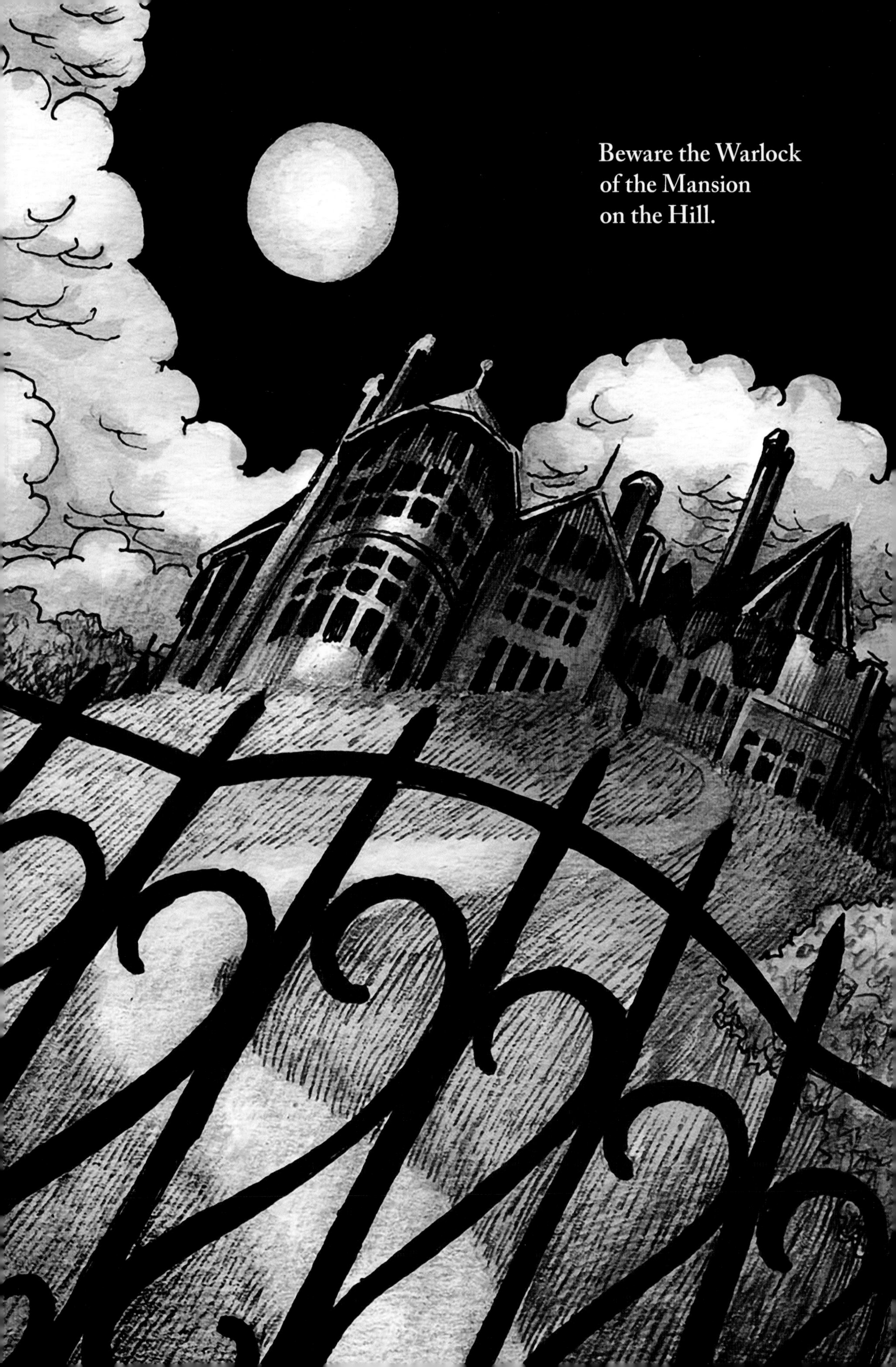

Beware the Warlock
of the Mansion
on the Hill.

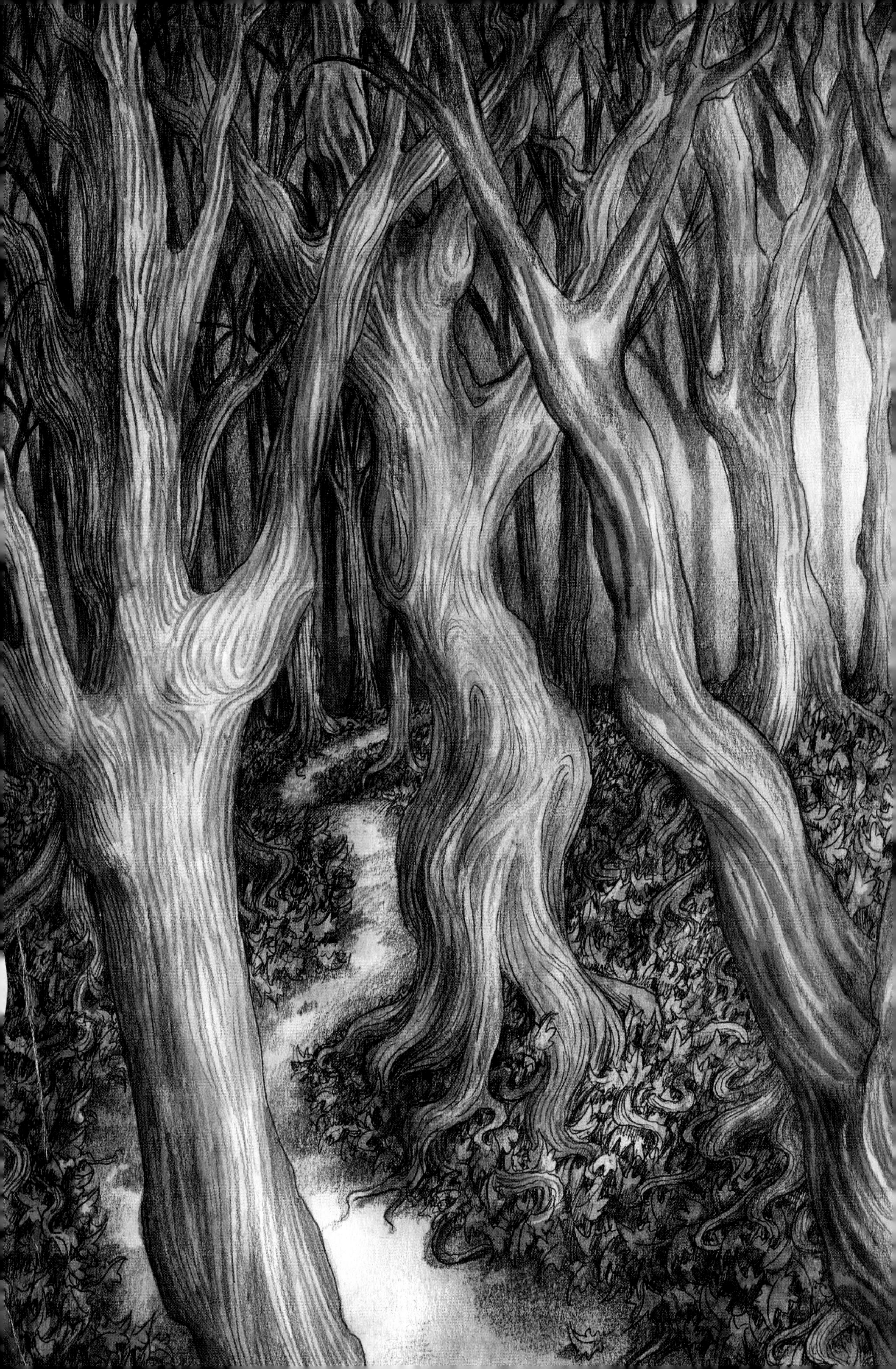